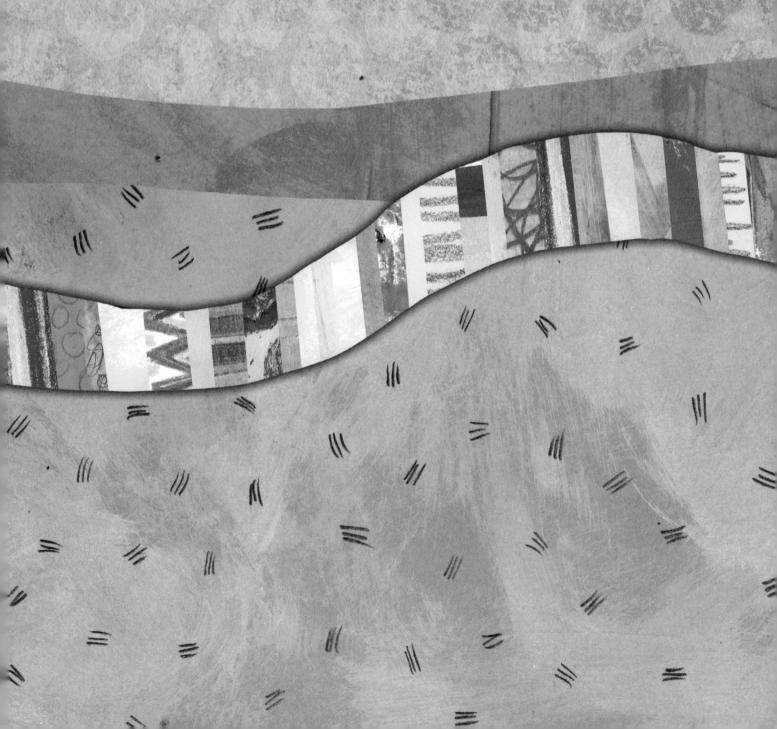

MW01011550

# 10 Minute Classics

Good books are some of the greatest treasures in the world. They can take you to incredible places and on fantastic adventures. So sit back with a 10 MINUTE CLASSIC and indulge a lifelong love for reading.

We cannot, however, guarantee your 10 minute break won't turn into 15, 20, or 30 minutes, as these FUN stories and engaging pictures will have you turning the pages AGAIN and AGAIN!

Designed by Flowerpot Press
in Franklin, TN.
www.FlowerpotPress.com
Designer: Stephanie Meyers
Editor: Katrine Crow
DJS-0912-0165
ISBN: 978-1-4867-1221-2
Made in China/Fabriqué en Chine

Copyright © 2017
Flowerpot Press, a Division of Kamalu LLC, Franklin, TN, U.S.A. and Flowerpot Children's Press, Inc., Oakville, ON, Canada. All rights reserved. No part of this publication may be reproduced, stored in a retrieval system or transmitted, in any form or by any means, electronic, mechanical, photocopying, recording, optical scan, or otherwise, without the prior written permission of the copyright holder.

This is the magical story of a girl named DOROTHY. In this story, DOROTHY takes a GREAT BIG ADVENTURE. This GREAT BIG ADVENTURE starts on a very small farm in KANSAS...

DOROTHY is a young orphan girl who has a little dog TOTO. TOTO is her BEST FRIEND. The BEST FRIENDS live in a very small farmhouse, on a very small farm, in a very small town, on a VERY BIG PRAIRIE, where very little ever happens.

Very little, that is, until one day when the BEST FRIENDS were home alone and a HUMONGOUS cyclone blew through the prairie. The HUMONGOUS cyclone picked up the very small farmhouse and took it on a HUMONGOUS journey to a land that was very far away. The land was OZ.

When taking a journey in your house, it is IMPORTANT to note there is no way to steer. Your house goes where the wind blows.

DOROTHY'S house blew all the way to OZ...

...where it landed right on top of the WICKED WITCH of the East. Dorothy thought this was pretty bad. The MUNCHKINS who lived there thought this was pretty good. The MUNCHKINS had been ruled by the WICKED WITCH, who was evil, so they were very happy to be freed from her control.

The MUNCHKINS, along with the GOOD WITCH of the North, rewarded Dorothy with a pair of MAGICAL RUBY SHOES.

DOROTHY just wanted to go home to KANSAS.

"How do I get home to KANSAS?" she asked.

"Follow the road of YELLOW bricks," said the GOOD WITCH. "It will lead to the EMERALD CITY, where there lives a WIZARD. The WIZARD can get you back home."

So off DOROTHY went, followed closely by her BEST FRIEND TOTO.

When traveling a road of YELLOW bricks in a land filled with WITCHES and MUNCHKINS, you should be prepared for many NEW and DIFFERENT adventures and characters. On their journey, DOROTHY and TOTO met three wonderful characters who became their FRIENDS...

First, they met the SCARECROW, who was just hanging out. REALLY. He was hanging from a pole in a field. DOROTHY rescued him from the field and the THREE FRIENDS headed on down the road.

Next, they met the TIN WOODMAN, who was a stiff.
REALLY. He was rusted so badly that his joints were
stiff. DOROTHY loosened his limbs with oil and the
FOUR FRIENDS headed on down the road.

Next, they met the COWARDLY LION, who was struck by
DOROTHY. REALLY. He tried to scare the FRIENDS, so DOROTHY
slapped him, at which point he admitted he was a coward, said
he was sorry, and the FIVE FRIENDS headed on down the road.

The FRIENDS all followed the road to the EMERALD CITY where they hoped to meet the WIZARD. The SCARECROW hoped the WIZARD would give him BRAINS. The TIN WOODMAN hoped the WIZARD would give him a HEART. The COWARDLY LION hoped the WIZARD would give him COURAGE. DOROTHY and TOTO just wanted to go home to KANSAS...

When the five FRIENDS arrived at the EMERALD CITY, they went in search of the WIZARD. When they found him, he quickly agreed to help each of them. Even more quickly, he set a CONDITION for his help:

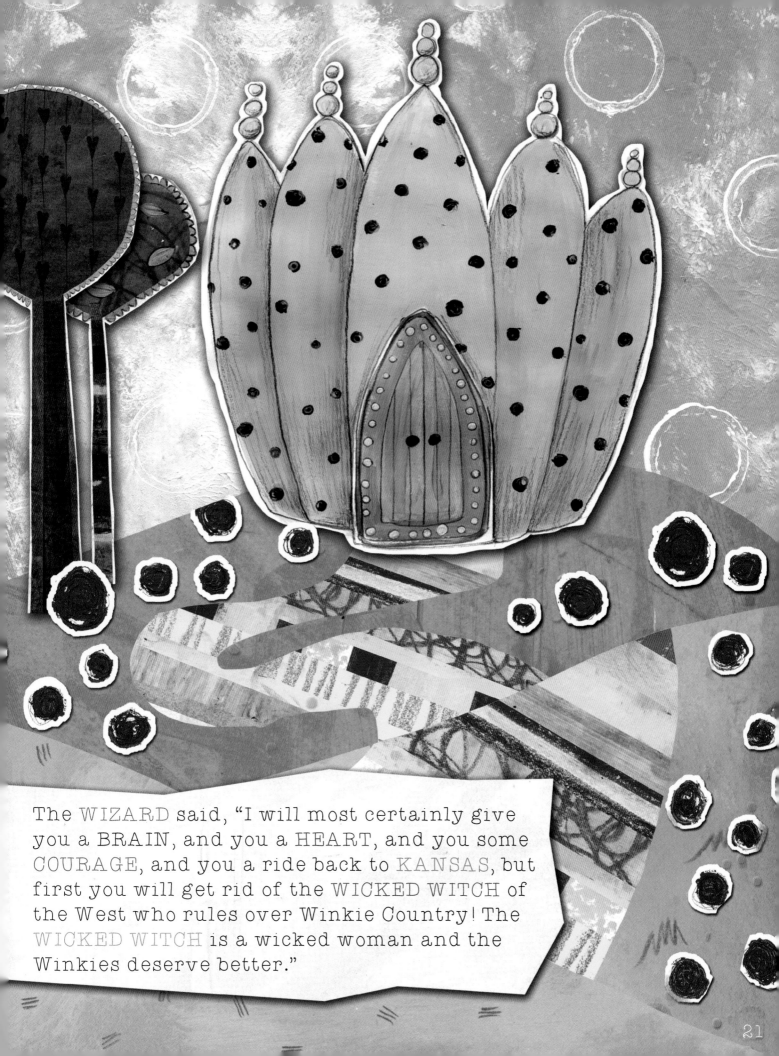

The WIZARD said, "I will most certainly give you a BRAIN, and you a HEART, and you some COURAGE, and you a ride back to KANSAS, but first you will get rid of the WICKED WITCH of the West who rules over Winkie Country! The WICKED WITCH is a wicked woman and the Winkies deserve better."

As the FRIENDS wandered Winkie
Country in search of the WICKED WITCH,
they had many ADVENTURES and were
met with many CHALLENGES. It took all the
talents of all the FRIENDS to prevail.
Along the way, they
sometimes surprised
themselves...

turn
back
now!

haunted
forest
witch's
castle

SCARECROW was surprised that he was SMART.

TIN WOODMAN was surprised by his HEART.

COWARDLY LION was surprised by his BRAVERY.

And DOROTHY was surprised to find that all she needed was a PAIL OF WATER to rid the world of the WICKED WITCH of the West.

When the FRIENDS returned to the WIZARD to claim their
REWARD, they were even more surprised as the WIZARD
explained to them that all they had ever wanted was
already INSIDE them.

The WIZARD proclaimed:
"SCARECROW, you
have shown that you already
have BRAINS.

TIN WOODMAN, you
have shown that
you already
have a HEART.

COWARDLY LION,
you have shown
that you already
have COURAGE."

"What about me?" whispered DOROTHY.

29

While the WIZARD was making his declarations, and DOROTHY was nervously wondering about her own wish, the GOOD WITCH was watching and listening. When she heard DOROTHY, she spoke up:

*click.*

*click*

"DOROTHY, just like your FRIENDS, you have also always had what you needed. Those RUBY SHOES are MAGICAL and will take you home to KANSAS. Just CLICK your heels THREE times, make a WISH, and away you GO. But be sure to bring TOTO with you."

*click*

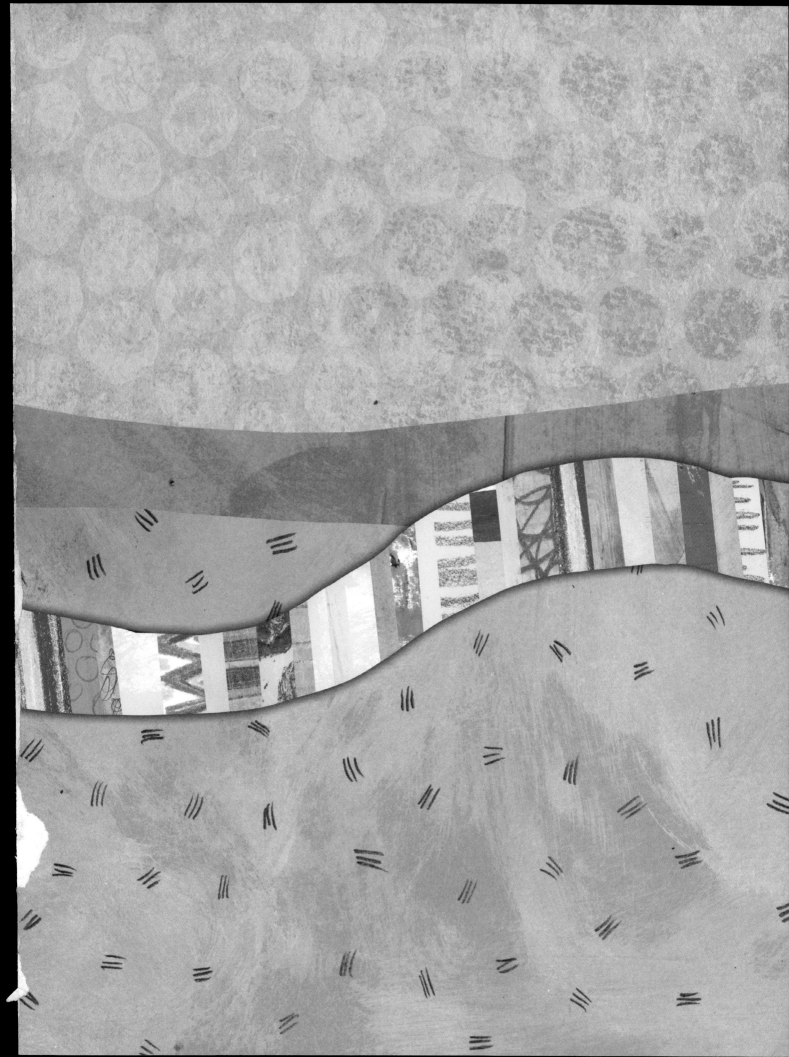